Hop, Joey, Hop!

by Miriam Sklar

ISBN: 978-1-338-75076-8
Illustrated by John Lund

Published by Scholastic Inc., 557 Broadway, New York, NY 10012

10 9 8 7 6 5 4 68 25 26 27/0

Printed in Jiaxing, China. First printing, January 2021.

Hop, Joey, hop!

Spin, Joey, spin!

Stand, Joey, stand!

Dance, Joey, dance!

Slide, Joey, slide!

Roll, Joey, roll!

Rest, Joey, rest!